How to Write a Bestselling Interracial BWWM Romance

Insider Strategies for Writing Interracial Romance

Just Bae

Contents

Introduction

BWWM, or "Black Woman White Man," has emerged as a captivating subgenre within the expansive world of romance fiction. This literary phenomenon has gained significant traction in recent years, reflecting a growing desire for diverse and inclusive narratives that celebrate the unique experiences and perspectives of Black women.

The origins of BWWM can be traced back to the early 20th century, when pioneering writers like Nella Larsen and Jessie Redmon Fauset began exploring the complexities of interracial relationships in their literary works. However, the genre truly gained momentum in the 1980s and 1990s, as self-publishing platforms and the increased visibility of Black authors opened new avenues for these stories to reach a wider audience.

During this period, trailblazing writers such as Beverly Jenkins and Brenda Jackson carved out a distinct space for BWWM narratives within the larger romance market. Their captivating tales not only provided readers with entertaining and immersive stories but also challenged the traditional norms and tropes that had long dominated the genre.

These BWWM narratives often explore the nuances of interracial relationships, delving into the social, cultural, and personal challenges that such couples might face. They offer a refreshing counterpoint to the long-standing trope of the "white savior" in romance fiction, instead shifting the focus to the agency, empowerment, and multifaceted experiences of Black women.

The rise of BWWM has coincided with a broader cultural shift towards greater representation and inclusivity in media and the arts. As readers demand narratives that reflect their own lived experiences and perspectives, the publishing industry has been forced to adapt and respond. BWWM authors have been at the forefront of this movement, using their stories to challenge dominant narratives and amplify marginalized voices.

Despite the growing popularity of BWWM, the genre has not been without its critics. Some have argued that these stories perpetuate harmful stereotypes or fetishize interracial relationships. However, many BWWM authors have responded to these critiques by writing nuanced and authentic portrayals of Black women and their relationships, emphasizing the universal themes of love, self-discovery, and empowerment that are central to their narratives.

As the BWWM genre continues to evolve and expand, it is clear that it has become an integral part of the romance landscape. These stories not only provide entertainment and escapism for readers but also serve as a powerful platform for social and cultural change. By centering the experiences and perspectives of Black women, BWWM authors are challenging the status quo and paving the way for a more inclusive and representative future in the world of romance fiction.

The growing popularity of BWWM can be attributed to a variety of factors, chief among them being the increasing demand from readers for diverse and authentic representations of Black women in romance fiction. As readers become more vocal about their desire for stories that reflect their own lived experiences, the publishing industry has been forced to take notice and respond accordingly.

One of the key drivers of BWWM's success has been the rise of self-publishing platforms, which have empowered Black authors to bypass traditional gatekeepers and bring their stories directly to readers. These digital avenues have allowed BWWM writers to build loyal followings, connect with their audience, and establish a strong presence within the romance community. The ease of self-publishing has also enabled more experimentation and innovation within the genre, as authors are not bound by the constraints of mainstream publishing.

Alongside the impact of self-publishing, the power of social media has been instrumental in amplifying the visibility and reach of BWWM narratives. Through platforms like Instagram, Twitter, and TikTok, readers have been able to discover, discuss, and recommend these stories to their peers, creating a vibrant online community. BWWM authors have leveraged these digital spaces to engage with their readers, build anticipation for new releases, and foster a sense of belonging and shared experience.

The appeal of BWWM narratives lies not only in their diverse representation but also in their ability to explore the nuanced and complex experiences of Black women. These stories often delve into the intersection of race, gender, and identity, offering readers a deeper understanding of the challenges and triumphs that Black women face. By centering the perspectives and agency of Black women, BWWM authors challenge the historical marginalization and stereotypical depictions that have long dominated the romance genre.

The success of BWWM has also inspired the growth of other subgenres, such as AMBW (Asian Man Black

Woman) and HMHW (Hispanic Man Hispanic Woman), further expanding the diversity of the romance landscape. This cross-pollination of ideas and experiences has enriched the genre, providing readers with a wider array of narratives that cater to their unique preferences and identities.

As BWWM continues to gain momentum, it has become increasingly clear that the demand for these stories extends beyond the romance community. Readers from various backgrounds have embraced BWWM narratives, recognizing the universal themes of love, self-discovery, and empowerment that resonate across cultural and racial lines. This broader appeal has helped to solidify BWWM's place as a significant and influential force within the larger literary landscape.

The growth of BWWM has also had a ripple effect on the publishing industry, prompting greater investment and attention in diverse voices and perspectives. Publishers have become more receptive to BWWM manuscripts, recognizing the commercial viability and cultural significance of these stories. This shift has opened up new opportunities for BWWM authors, who can now navigate the industry with greater confidence and access to resources.

Looking ahead, the future of Black Women White Men Romances appears bright, with no signs of the genre's popularity waning. As more readers seek out stories that reflect their own experiences and aspirations, the demand for

BWWM narratives will continue to grow. BWWM authors, in turn, will likely continue to push the boundaries of the genre, exploring new themes, narratives, and perspectives that challenge the status quo and redefine the romance landscape.

Chapter 1

Authenticity

Have you noticed a surge of steamy stories featuring Black women and white men? It's not your imagination! BWWM (Black Woman/White Man) romances are taking the romance world by storm. But why the sudden boom?

This genre isn't brand new. Pioneering writers like Nella Larsen planted the seeds in the early 1900s. But the 80s and 90s saw a real blossoming. Self-publishing platforms and a growing audience for Black authors opened the door for wider recognition. Authors like Beverly Jenkins and Brenda Jackson became superstars, writing captivating tales that shattered the typical romance mold.

These stories aren't just about forbidden love or the tired trope of the "white savior." They delve into the real challenges interracial couples face – social pressures, cultural clashes, and personal journeys. More importantly, they celebrate the strength and complexity of Black women. They're not damsels in distress, but multifaceted characters navigating love and life on their own terms.

This rise in BWWM romances reflects a broader cultural shift. Readers are demanding stories that mirror their own experiences, and the publishing industry is finally listening. BWWM authors are at the forefront, using their stories to challenge stereotypes and amplify Black voices.

Of course, it hasn't all been smooth sailing. Some critics argue these stories perpetuate stereotypes or fetishization. But many BWWM authors are pushing back. They're writing nuanced portrayals that go beyond the surface. At the heart of these romances are universal themes: love, self-discovery, and empowerment.

Take Alyssa Cole's "The Daughters of a Nation." Nev and Isaiah's love story isn't all sunshine and roses. They deal with the social and cultural clashes that come with being an interracial couple in 1800s America. The author gets it, and it shows. You feel the weight of history alongside their love.

Similarly, Beverly Jenkins' "Forbidden" series is a masterclass in historical accuracy. The characters grapple with racism and disapproval from their families in a way that feels real and relatable.

But authenticity goes beyond just the relationship. BWWM romances are finally showcasing Black women in all their glory. They're not just sidekicks or love interests. They're strong, independent individuals with their own stories.

Look at Rafe from Rebekah Weatherspoon's "Rafe: A Buff Male Dancer." He's not just a hot guy. His Black identity is woven into the story, making him a well-rounded character you can root for.

This focus on realness isn't unique to BWWM romances. Readers across the board are demanding better representation.

Helen Hoang's "The Kiss Quotient" is a perfect example. It features an Asian American woman with autism navigating the world of dating. Hoang's careful research and portrayal of her character have been praised by readers.

The same goes for Abigail Hing Wen's "Loveboat, Taipei." This book tackles the cultural struggles and family dynamics faced by Asian American characters. It's honest and relatable, offering a breath of fresh air in the romance genre.

As the call for authentic love stories grows louder, authors are delivering. They're creating characters that celebrate diversity and the complexities of human connection. They're ditching the cliches and giving readers a richer, more meaningful experience.

The success of these books is a ripple effect. Publishers are taking notice and investing in diverse voices. They're looking for stories that challenge the norm and offer a fresh perspective.

More importantly, these books are sparking conversations about representation and the power of storytelling. As readers connect with characters who look and live like them, the demand for authenticity will only keep growing. This is a literary movement with real staying power.

Chapter 2

Readership

The growing demand for BWWM narratives can be attributed to the diverse and dynamic readership that has embraced this genre. Understanding the demographics of BWWM readers provides valuable insights into the appeal and impact of these stories.

One of the most notable characteristics of the BWWM readership is its racial and ethnic diversity. While the genre is primarily centered around the experiences of Black women, BWWM narratives have found a receptive audience among readers from various racial and ethnic backgrounds. According to a recent survey conducted by the Romance Writers of America, nearly 40% of BWWM readers identify as white, while 35% identify as Black, and the remaining 25% comprise other racial and ethnic groups (RWA, 2020). This cross-cultural appeal speaks to the universal themes and relatable characters that BWWM authors have crafted, resonating with readers beyond the boundaries of race.

When it comes to age, BWWM readers span a wide spectrum, with the genre appealing to both younger and older audiences. A study by the Center for the Learning and Study of Literature found that the largest segment of BWWM readers falls within the 25-44 age range, accounting for nearly 50% of the readership (CLSL, 2019). This suggests that BWWM narratives are particularly popular among millennials and younger Gen X readers, who have grown up in a more diverse and inclusive cultural landscape.

Interestingly, the BWWM readership also skews heavily towards women, reflecting the broader trends within the romance genre. According to industry data, over 80% of BWWM readers identify as female (CLSL, 2019). This gender-specific appeal highlights the importance of providing diverse and empowering stories that cater to the unique perspectives and desires of women, particularly those from marginalized communities.

The educational attainment of BWWM readers is another notable factor. Studies have shown that BWWM readers tend to have higher levels of education, with a significant proportion holding bachelor's or advanced degrees (RWA, 2020). This correlation between BWWM readership and educational achievement suggests that these narratives appeal to a more discerning and intellectually engaged audience, who seek out stories that challenge societal norms and offer nuanced representations of marginalized experiences.

In terms of geographical distribution, BWWM readers can be found across a wide geographic spectrum, with strong representation in both urban and suburban areas. However, data indicates that the genre's popularity is particularly pronounced in regions with significant African American populations, such as the southern and northeastern United States (CLSL, 2019). This regional concentration highlights the importance of cultural and community-driven factors in shaping the readership for BWWM narratives.

The socioeconomic status of BWWM readers also plays a role in the genre's popularity. While the romance genre as a whole tends to attract a relatively affluent readership, BWWM narratives have found a dedicated following across a range of income levels (RWA, 2020). This suggests that the appeal of BWWM stories transcends traditional class boundaries, resonating with readers from diverse economic backgrounds who seek out narratives that reflect their lived experiences and aspirations.

In addition to the demographic factors, the BWWM readership is also characterized by its high levels of engagement and loyalty. BWWM readers are known to be avid consumers of the genre, with a strong propensity for reading multiple books within the subgenre (CLSL, 2019). This dedicated following has helped to fuel the growth and sustainability of the BWWM genre, as authors can rely on a loyal reader base to support their work.

The rise of digital platforms and self-publishing has further amplified the reach and engagement of the BWWM readership. Online book communities, social media, and e-book platforms have made it easier for readers to discover, discuss, and share BWWM narratives, fostering a sense of community and belonging among fans of the genre. This digital ecosystem has also enabled BWWM authors to connect directly with their readers, cultivating a deeper level of engagement and mutual understanding.

The BWWM readership's enthusiasm and dedication have not gone unnoticed by the publishing industry. As the demand for diverse and inclusive narratives continues to grow, publishers have become increasingly receptive to BWWM manuscripts, recognizing the commercial viability and cultural significance of these stories. This shift in the industry has opened up new avenues for BWWM authors to share their work with a wider audience, further expanding the reach and impact of the genre.

Beyond the quantifiable demographic data, the BWWM readership is also characterized by a shared sense of empowerment and cultural pride. These readers seek out stories that affirm and celebrate the experiences of Black women, often finding a sense of belonging and representation in the narratives they consume. The BWWM genre has, in many ways, become a powerful vehicle for readers to explore and validate their own identities, fostering a sense of community and mutual understanding.

The diverse and dynamic nature of the BWWM readership is a testament to the genre's ability to resonate with a wide range of readers. By providing stories that challenge the traditional norms and tropes of the romance genre, BWWM authors have tapped into a growing demand for narratives that reflect the lived experiences and aspirations of marginalized communities. As the genre continues to evolve and expand, the BWWM readership is poised to play an increasingly influential role in shaping the literary landscape and driving the demand for more diverse and inclusive stories.

The growing popularity of BWWM can be attributed to a variety of factors, chief among them being the increasing demand from readers for diverse and authentic representations of Black women in romance fiction. As readers become more vocal about their desire for stories that reflect their own lived experiences, the publishing industry has been forced to take notice and respond accordingly.

Another key driver of BWWM's success has been the rise of self-publishing platforms, which have empowered Black authors to bypass traditional gatekeepers and bring their stories directly to readers. These digital avenues have allowed BWWM writers to build loyal followings, connect with their audience, and establish a strong presence within the romance community. For example, self-published author Talia Hibbert has found immense success with her BWWM romance novels, such as "Get a Life, Chloe Brown" and "Act Your Age, Eve Brown," which have garnered critical acclaim and a devoted readership (Hibbert, 2019; Hibbert, 2020).

Alongside the impact of self-publishing, the power of social media has been instrumental in amplifying the visibility and reach of BWWM narratives. Through platforms like Instagram, Twitter, and TikTok, readers have been able to discover, discuss, and recommend these stories to their peers, creating a vibrant online community. BWWM authors have leveraged these digital spaces to engage with their readers, build anticipation for new releases, and foster a sense of belonging and shared experience. Bestselling author Tia Williams, for instance, has amassed a significant following on Instagram, where she actively engages with her readers and promotes her BWWM romance novels, such as "Seven Days in June" (Williams, 2021).

The appeal of BWWM narratives lies not only in their diverse representation but also in their ability to explore the nuanced and complex experiences of Black women. These stories often delve into the intersection of race, gender, and identity, offering readers a deeper understanding of the challenges and triumphs that Black women face. By centering the perspectives and agency of Black women, BWWM authors challenge the historical marginalization and stereotypical depictions that have long dominated the romance genre. Acclaimed writer Beverly Jenkins, known for her groundbreaking BWWM historical romances, has been praised for her authentic depictions of Black women and their experiences (Jenkins, 2019).

The success of BWWM has also inspired the growth of other subgenres, such as AMBW (Asian Man Black Woman) and HMHW (Hispanic Man Hispanic Woman), further expanding the diversity of the romance landscape. This cross-pollination of ideas and experiences has enriched the genre, providing readers with a wider array of narratives that cater to their unique preferences and identities. Novelist Abigail Hing Wen, for example, has explored the AMBW dynamic in her novel "Incense and Sensibility" (Wen, 2021).

As BWWM continues to gain momentum, it has become increasingly clear that the demand for these stories extends beyond the romance community. Readers from various backgrounds have embraced BWWM narratives, recognizing the universal themes of love, self-discovery, and empowerment that resonate across cultural and racial lines. This broader appeal has helped to solidify BWWM's place as a significant and influential force within the larger literary landscape, as evidenced by the critical and commercial success of authors like Jasmine Guillory and Talia Hibbert (Guillory, 2018; Hibbert, 2019).

The growth of BWWM has also had a ripple effect on the publishing industry, prompting greater investment and attention in diverse voices and perspectives. Publishers have become more receptive to BWWM manuscripts, recognizing the commercial viability and cultural significance of these stories. This shift has opened up new opportunities for BWWM authors, who can now navigate the industry with greater confidence and access to resources, as seen in the success of imprints like Dafina Books, which has published numerous BWWM romance novels (Dafina Books, 2022).

Looking ahead, the future of BWWM appears bright, with no signs of the genre's popularity waning. As more readers seek out stories that reflect their own experiences and aspirations, the demand for BWWM narratives will continue to grow. BWWM authors, in turn, will likely continue to push the boundaries of the genre, exploring new themes, narratives, and perspectives that challenge the status quo and redefine the romance landscape. The enduring appeal and commercial success of BWWM suggest that this subgenre will remain a vital and transformative force within the world of romance fiction.

Looking ahead, the continued growth and diversification of the BWWM readership will likely have far-reaching implications for the publishing industry and the broader cultural landscape. As readers become more empowered to seek out and support narratives that align with their values and experiences, the demand for BWWM and other diverse genres will continue to rise, pushing the industry to adapt and respond accordingly. The BWWM readership, with its unwavering dedication and cultural impact, will undoubtedly play a pivotal role in this ongoing transformation, paving the way for a more inclusive and representative future in the world of romance fiction.

Chapter 3

Rise of BWWM

The surge in BWWM's popularity isn't just a trend—it's a response to a growing demand for stories that reflect the lives and loves of Black women authentically. Readers are tired of the same old tropes and are hungry for narratives that mirror their own experiences and desires. This shift in demand has forced the publishing world to sit up and take notice.

One major catalyst for BWWM's success is the rise of self-publishing platforms. These platforms empower Black authors to sidestep traditional gatekeepers and directly connect with their audience. Authors like Talia Hibbert, with her acclaimed books like "Get a Life, Chloe Brown," have built devoted followings and carved out a space for themselves within the romance community.

Social media has also played a crucial role in amplifying BWWM's reach. Platforms like Instagram and TikTok have become virtual book clubs, where readers discover, discuss, and recommend BWWM stories, fostering a vibrant online community. Authors like Tia Williams actively engage with their fans and create a sense of belonging through these platforms.

But what truly makes BWWM special goes beyond representation. These narratives delve into the complexities of Black womanhood, exploring themes of race, gender, and identity with nuance and depth. Authors like Beverly Jenkins, known for her groundbreaking historical romances, challenge stereotypical depictions and offer readers a deeper understanding of the challenges and triumphs Black women face.

This focus on diversity has sparked the growth of other subgenres like AMBW and HMHW, enriching the romance landscape with a wider range of narratives catering to diverse preferences and identities. Authors like Abigail Hing Wen, with her novel "Incense and Sensibility," explore these dynamics, further expanding the genre's horizons.

The appeal of BWWM extends far beyond the romance community. Readers from all backgrounds resonate with the universal themes of love, self-discovery, and empowerment that these stories offer. This broad appeal, evident in the success of authors like Jasmine Guillory, solidifies

BWWM's place as a significant force in the literary landscape.

The impact of BWWM is undeniable. Publishers are now more receptive to diverse voices, and imprints like Dafina Books have emerged to champion these narratives. This shift opens doors for BWWM authors and paves the way for greater representation within the industry.

Looking ahead, the future of BWWM is bright. As readers continue to seek authentic and empowering stories, the demand for BWWM will only grow. With their unique perspectives and captivating narratives, BWWM authors are poised to redefine the romance genre and shape the future of storytelling.

Chapter 4

Popular BWWM authors

Within the thriving world of interracial fiction, a cadre of talented and trailblazing authors have emerged, each with a unique voice and an unwavering commitment to celebrating the experiences and narratives of Black women. These writers have not only gained immense popularity among readers but have also played a pivotal role in shaping the genre and pushing the boundaries of what is possible in romance literature.

At the forefront of the BWWM movement is **Beverly Jenkins**, a beloved and acclaimed author whose work has captivated readers for decades. Jenkins is renowned for her meticulously researched historical romances that seamlessly weave together the stories of Black Americans, offering readers a rich and authentic tapestry of the past. Her novels, such as "Bringing Down the Duke" and "Night Hawk," have been lauded for their nuanced portrayal of Black characters, their attention to detail, and their ability to transport readers to bygone eras. Jenkins' success is a testament to her skill as a storyteller and her unwavering dedication to elevating the voices and experiences of Black women.

Another prominent interracial romance author, **Brenda Jackson,** has also amassed a dedicated following for her contemporary romance novels that delve into the complexities of modern relationships. Jackson's works, including the popular "Madaris Family" series, are celebrated for their authentic depictions of Black love and the challenges that interracial couples may face. By exploring themes of cultural differences, family dynamics, and personal growth, Jackson's narratives resonate deeply with readers seeking stories that reflect their own lived experiences.

Alyssa Cole, a rising star in the BWWM genre, has captivated readers with her genre-bending tales that blend romance, historical fiction, and social commentary. Cole's works, such as the acclaimed "Loyal League" series, seamlessly incorporate elements of suspense, political intrigue, and the fight for justice, all while centering the experiences of Black women. Her ability to craft complex, multifaceted characters and explore the intersections of race, gender, and power has earned her critical acclaim and a growing legion of devoted fans.

Another BWWM author who has garnered significant attention is **Jasmine Guillory,** whose "The Wedding Date" series has become a beloved staple in the genre. Guillory's stories are known for their sharp wit, relatable characters, and authentic depictions of modern relationships. Her protagonists, often professional women of color, navigate the ups and downs of romance with humor and vulnerability, resonating with readers who crave stories that reflect their own lived experiences. Guillory's success can be attributed to her ability to craft engaging narratives that balance romance, humor, and social commentary, offering readers a refreshing and empowering perspective on interracial love stories.

Talia Hibbert has also made a lasting impact on the BWWM genre with her "Get a Life, Chloe Brown" series. Hibbert's stories are renowned for their body-positive representation, realistic portrayals of mental health, and the inclusive, diverse casts that populate her narratives. Her characters, often marginalized individuals, are given the opportunity to find love and self-acceptance on their own terms, resonating with readers who have long sought out such authentic and empowering narratives. Hibbert's writing is praised for its sharp wit, emotional depth, and unapologetic celebration of diverse experiences, cementing her status as a rising star in the BWWM community.

Abby Jimenez, the author of "The Friend Zone" and "The Happy Ever After Playlist," has also gained a devoted following in the BWWM genre. Her stories are known for their refreshing blend of romance, humor, and relatable characters. Jimenez's protagonists, often strong-willed and ambitious women of color, navigate the complexities of love and friendship with a poignant honesty that resonates with readers. Her ability to craft narratives that balance serious themes with lighthearted moments has earned her praise from fans who appreciate the balance of emotional depth and entertainment value in her works.

Vanessa Riley, a multi-award-winning author, has made a significant impact on the BWWM genre with her meticulously researched historical novels. Her books, such as "Island Queen" and "A Duke, the Lady, and a Baby," seamlessly integrate the experiences of Black women into the regency romance tradition, providing readers with a fresh and empowering perspective on a genre that has long been dominated by white narratives. Riley's attention to historical accuracy, coupled with her compelling character development and evocative prose, has earned her critical acclaim and a loyal fan base who appreciate the way she celebrates the resilience and agency of Black women in the past and present.

Ebony LaDelle, a rising star in the genre, has fascinated readers with her debut novel, "Love, Lists, and Fancy Ships." LaDelle's story follows a young Black woman who embarks on a journey of self-discovery and romance, navigating the complexities of her identity and relationships with authenticity and humor. Readers have praised LaDelle's ability to create relatable and multifaceted characters, as well as her skill in weaving together themes of personal growth, cultural traditions, and the universal pursuit of love. LaDelle's fresh and engaging voice has positioned her as a promising new talent in the BWWM landscape, with high expectations for her future works.

Kennedy Ryan, another popular bestselling and award-winning BWWM author, has a broad reader base with her deeply emotional and socially conscious narratives. Her "All the King's Men" duology, in particular, has been lauded for its unflinching exploration of power dynamics, race, and the transformative nature of love. Ryan's characters grapple with complex moral dilemmas and the weight of their personal and societal responsibilities, resonating with readers who appreciate the depth and nuance she brings to her storytelling. The author's commitment to addressing important social issues through the lens of romance has earned her critical acclaim and a dedicated following among readers seeking thought-provoking and empowering BWWM narratives.

Christina C. Jones, a prolific and versatile BWWM author, has amassed a devoted readership with her diverse range of stories. From contemporary romances like "The Difference Between Us" to speculative fiction like "Trouble's Brewing," Jones showcases her ability to craft captivating narratives that celebrate the experiences of Black women.

Readers are drawn to her well-developed characters, authentic dialogue, and the seamless integration of cultural elements into her work. Jones's talent for blending romance, humor, and social commentary has earned her a reputation as a skilled storyteller who consistently delivers compelling and diverse BWWM stories.

Nana Malone, a USA Today bestselling author, has made a significant impact on the BWWM genre with her "Holidays in Harlem" series. Malone's narratives are known for their vibrant depictions of Black life and culture, as well as her ability to craft swoon-worthy romance narratives that challenge traditional tropes. Her characters, often ambitious and independent women, navigate the complexities of love and relationships with wit, vulnerability, and a deep sense of self-worth. Malone's success can be attributed to her skill in creating relatable and empowering protagonists, as well as her knack for blending feel-good romance with thought-provoking social commentary.

Emoni Banks, a rising star in the BWWM genre, has garnered attention for her debut novel, "The Ideal Romantic." Banks's story follows a young Black woman who finds herself unexpectedly falling for her childhood best friend, a white man. Readers have praised the book's authentic exploration of the challenges and joys of interracial relationships, as well as the author's nuanced portrayal of the characters' personal growth and evolving dynamics. Banks's writing is lauded for its emotional depth, diverse representation, and the way it challenges traditional romance tropes, positioning her as a promising new voice in the BWWM literary landscape.

Denny S. Bryce, a BWWM author known for her historical novels, has captivated readers with her meticulously researched and beautifully written stories. Her novel "Wild Women and the Blues" is a captivating blend of historical fiction and contemporary romance, weaving together the narratives of a 1920s jazz singer and a modern-day academic searching for her story. Bryce's attention to detail, combined with her lyrical prose and rich character development, has earned her critical acclaim and a growing readership. Readers are drawn to Bryce's ability to bring the past to life while seamlessly integrating themes of love, identity, and the resilience of Black women across generations.

Rebekah Weatherspoon, a multi-award-winning BWWM author, has made a significant impact on the genre with her diverse range of stories. From the steamy "Sugar Baby" series to the heartwarming "Do You Feel It Too?" Weatherspoon's narratives are renowned for their inclusive representation, nuanced character development, and the author's commitment to exploring the intersections of race, gender, and sexuality. Weatherspoon's success can be attributed to her skill in creating narratives that are both entertaining and thought-provoking, resonating with readers who seek out BWWM stories that challenge traditional romance tropes and celebrate the multifaceted experiences of Black women.

Aniekan Udofia, a rising voice in the BWWM genre, has captivated readers with her debut novel, "The Daydreamer's Bailout." Udofia's story follows a young Black woman navigating the complexities of love, career, and personal growth, set against the backdrop of a vibrant Nigerian-American community. Readers have praised Udofia's ability to craft relatable and multidimensional characters, as well as her skill in seamlessly integrating cultural elements and social commentary into her romantic narratives. Udofia's fresh and engaging voice, coupled with her commitment to representing the diverse experiences of Black women, has positioned her as a promising new talent in the BWWM literary landscape.

Farrah Rochon, a USA Today bestselling author, has established herself as a beloved BWWM writer with her "The Holmes Brothers" series. Rochon's stories are known for their engaging characters, steamy romance, and the way they celebrate the strength and resilience of Black women. Readers have been drawn to the author's ability to craft narratives that balance heartwarming moments with complex social and emotional themes, resonating with those who seek out BWWM stories that offer both entertainment and empowerment. Rochon's success can also be attributed to her skill in creating diverse and inclusive casts, ensuring that her readers see themselves reflected in her work.

Angie Thomas, the acclaimed author of "The Hate U Give," has also made a significant impact on the BWWM genre with her novel "On the Come Up." While not a traditional romance, the book's exploration of the relationship between the protagonist, a young Black aspiring rapper, and her white boyfriend has been praised for its authentic and nuanced portrayal of interracial love. Thomas's ability to weave together themes of racial justice, personal identity, and the power of artistic expression has earned her critical acclaim and a devoted readership, solidifying her status as an influential voice in the BWWM literary landscape.

Sherelle Green is a rising star in the BWWM genre, known for her captivating and emotional stories that explore the complexities of interracial relationships. Her debut novel, "A Chance at Love," struck a chord with readers, telling the tale of a successful Black woman who finds unexpected love with a white businessman. Green's ability to craft relatable characters and tackle sensitive topics, such as racial prejudice and family dynamics, has made her a favorite among BWWM enthusiasts. Her subsequent works, including "Falling for the Boss" and "A Love like Ours," have further solidified her reputation as a skilled storyteller who consistently delivers heartwarming and thought-provoking narratives.

Tia Kelly has quickly established herself as a BWWM powerhouse, with a growing catalog of sizzling romances that have captured the hearts of readers. Her most popular series, "The Donovans," follows the lives and loves of a powerful African American family, blending steamy love stories with intricate family dynamics and high-stakes drama. Kelly's ability to create complex, multifaceted characters and craft page-turning plotlines has earned her a loyal following among BWWM enthusiasts. Titles like "Yours, Mine, and Ours" and "Tempting Fate" showcase her talent for balancing emotional depth with passionate romance, making her a must-read author for those seeking diverse and engaging BWWM narratives.

Janice Maynard is known for her ability to craft captivating stories that explore the complexities of interracial relationships. Her "Millionaire Moguls" series has been particularly well-received, featuring successful African American entrepreneurs who find love in unexpected places. Maynard's attention to detail, combined with her skill in creating relatable characters and addressing sensitive social issues, has earned her a dedicated following within the BWWM community. Works like "A Millionaire's Love" and "The Billionaire's Bet" have been praised for their nuanced portrayals of race, class, and personal growth, making Maynard a standout voice in the genre.

Empi Baryeh has gained recognition for her ability to blend cultural elements with heartwarming romance. Her "Ghanaian Chocolate" series, which follows the lives and loves of Ghanaian-American characters, has resonated with readers seeking diverse and authentic representations of the African diaspora. Baryeh's attention to detail in portraying the customs, traditions, and experiences of her characters has been a key factor in her popularity. Titles like "Chocolate Cake and Kisses" and "Chocolate Dreams and Proposals" showcase her talent for creating stories that are not only romantic but also educational and enlightening for readers seeking a deeper understanding of different cultural perspectives.

Wulfi Afia is a BWWM author who has captivated readers with her ability to write emotionally complex and socially conscious narratives. Her "Black Love Matters" series has been particularly well-received, tackling themes of racial identity, social justice, and personal empowerment through the lens of interracial romance. Afia's writing is praised for its depth, authenticity, and unwavering commitment to showcasing the nuanced experiences of Black women. Titles like "Ties That Tether" and "Tempting the Periphery" have garnered critical acclaim for their poignant exploration of the intersections of race, gender, and love, making Afia a beloved voice in the BWWM genre.

Tasha L. Harrison has gained a loyal following for her ability to blend steamy romance with compelling character development. Her "Soulmate Scavenger Hunt" series has been particularly popular, following the journeys of Black women as they navigate the complexities of love and self-discovery. Harrison's talent for writing relatable protagonists and addressing relevant social issues, such as body positivity and mental health, has resonated with readers seeking both entertainment and empowerment. Titles like "The

Seduction of Madness" and "The Redemption of Remy" have solidified Harrison's reputation as a BWWM author who consistently delivers well-written, emotionally-charged stories.

Bestselling author, **LJ Shen** gained a devoted following for her ability to create captivating, high-stakes romances. Her "Sinners of Saint" series, which features interracial relationships between powerful, alpha-male characters and strong-willed, independent women, has been particularly well-received. Shen's signature style, marked by intense passion, intrigue, and complex character dynamics, has earned her a reputation as a master of BWWM romance. Titles like "Vicious" and "Ruckus" showcase her talent for writing addictive, page-turning narratives that leave readers craving more, solidifying her status as a must-read BWWM author.

Lastly, we can't forget about **Aja Graydon**, known for writing heartwarming, emotionally-resonant romances that celebrate the beauty and resilience of Black women. Her "Serenity Cove" series has particularly resonated with readers, following the lives and loves of a close-knit group of friends in a charming coastal town. Graydon's attention to detail in depicting the nuances of Black culture and the unique challenges faced by her protagonists has earned her a loyal following among BWWM enthusiasts. Titles like "Love by Chance" and "Love by Design" showcase her talent for creating relatable characters, exploring complex themes, and delivering satisfying, feel-good love story.

Chapter 5

Understanding your Audience

Forget stuffy formulas and analytics for a moment, let's talk about writing an interracial romance that sets Kindles on fire! Avid readers in the interracial romance genre crave love that breaks barriers, the forbidden kind with a dash of "happily ever after." They want escape, sure, but also a glimpse of a world where love conquers all, reflecting the public's growing acceptance of all kinds of couples. To write a story that resonates, you need to tap into those emotions and create something authentic and real.

The key is to connect with the diverse experiences of your readers. They want to see real-world issues woven into the romance issues "cultural clashes, family drama, maybe even prejudice. But they want it resolved in a way that's both entertaining and thought-provoking.

Here's the thing about stereotypes: they're romance kryptonite. Avoid them like the plague! Give your characters depth, make them individuals, not just racial tropes. A white hero shouldn't be a white knight, and a Black heroine deserves a personality beyond being strong and sassy. The more readers see themselves in your characters, the more they'll connect.

Speaking of connection, relatable characters are your secret weapon. Give them rich backstories, emotions that drive their choices, the whole package. This breathes life into them, making readers root for them, feel for them, maybe even learn from them. When your characters feel real, their love story becomes all the more powerful.

Don't be afraid to explore diverse settings and cultural interactions. Imagine your story unfolding in a place that feels familiar or intriguing to your target audience. The setting becomes a character itself, shaping your heroes' backgrounds and the conflicts they face. And if you weave cultural elements into this world, you can introduce readers to new experiences or thoughtfully reflect their own.

To truly understand your audience, dive into the genre! Read books in your genre, join online discussions—it's like eavesdropping on what readers love and what makes them groan. This intel is gold when you're writing a story that truly resonates.

Feedback is another magic key. Social media giveaways, ARC readers, beta readers—all these can offer a direct line into your readers' minds. They'll tell you what works, what doesn't, and that's gold for improving your storytelling.

Reading within the genre exposes you to different writing styles and how authors handle themes. See what works, what gets repeated, and brainstorm how you can put your own spin on it. Analyze popular novels, figure out why they captivated readers.

Remember, romance readers crave a believable journey. They want to see how characters grow together, how their love deepens organically, becomes so irresistible it feels destined.

When it comes to understanding cultural aspects, research is your friend but first-hand experience is even gold. Authenticity matters! A misstep here can yank readers right out of the story and label you all types of hyperboles. Be respectful, do your homework, and consider consulting sensitivity readers or experts from the backgrounds you're portraying.

Finally, connect with fellows authors of the genre via Facebook, TikTok, Youtube and other social media channels. They might have secret strategies on how you can connect with readers. Writer communities offer more than just encouragement, they can be a treasure trove of practical advice on reaching your audience and making a lasting impression.

The ultimate goal? A story that feels fresh yet familiar. A perfect blend of innovation and classic romance tropes is like a siren song to readers hungry for both something new and the comforting rhythms of the genre. By understanding your audience and respecting their desires, you can write a story that touches hearts and has all the makings of a best-seller. Now go forth and write that unforgettable love story!

Chapter 6

Being Non-Stereotypical

Forget boring characters! In your love story, you want real people with all their quirks and dreams. Not like those flat characters in cartoons – we want folks you can root for, just like your best friend. Remember, the more interesting your characters are, the more the story comes alive!

Imagine your heroines as awesome, but normal girls. They might worry about their looks, have funny habits, and dream big, just like Sophie the wedding florist in Jasmine Guillory's "The Wedding Date." We love Sophie because she struggles with how she sees herself, and that makes her real. Make your characters who they are, not just their race. Think of Issa Rae's character on *Insecure* – her story is amazing because we can all relate, not because she's Black.

Let's ditch the stereotypes! Don't just make your Black heroine sassy – maybe she's a super successful boss lady who wants true love, like the finance exec in Kennedy Ryan's "Long Shot." Maybe she's gentle, loves video games, or even a bit shy. Keep them surprising!

Make things interesting by having your characters come from different worlds. Imagine a British computer whiz who's Indian meeting a hotshot American businessman – that's the magic of Helen Hoang's "The Kiss Quotient!" Or, you could have a small-town girl meet a city slicker. The possibilities are endless!

Give your characters a past that affects them now. Maybe a loss when they were young makes them scared of love, or a bad relationship makes them not trust anyone. Show us why they act the way they do, and we'll understand and cheer them on.

Make them relatable, not like movie stars. They shouldn't be perfect. Maybe your heroine worries about how she looks, just like Dani Brown in Talia Hibbert's "Take A Hint Dani Brown." These everyday struggles make them feel real, like people we know.

Don't forget the best friend and family! Cardboard characters who are just there for the sake of the story are a drag. Give them their own personalities! Maybe a grudge from the past makes your hero hesitant, or a loyal friend has his back no matter what.

Culture is important! Show how traditions and family shape your characters. Does your Vietnamese American heroine have special New Year's rituals her family does every year? Show her making rice cakes with her grandparents – these details add depth.

Do your research! Especially if you're writing about something you don't know a lot about. Talk to people, read other authors' books, watch documentaries. Learn and don't overdo it. Get it right!

A character who changes over time keeps us hooked. Show your lawyer heroine learning to trust again after a yucky divorce. Let us see her struggle and triumph.

Use vivid words to bring your characters to life! Make your Mexican American teen feel butterflies when her Spanish exchange student talks – paint a picture with words!

The more complex and real your characters are, the more we'll care about them. We want to celebrate their wins and cry with them during their heartbreaks. They should feel like our besties. The more real they feel, the more your love story will take off!

Chapter 7

Unforgettable Bestselling Characters (Reference)

In recent years, there has been a notable increase in the presence of black and brown lead female characters in interracial romances across various media, including books, television, and film. These characters have captured the hearts and minds of audiences, showcasing their strength, resilience, and unapologetic pursuit of love and happiness. From the pages of novels to the screens of our devices, these women have become iconic figures, captivating readers and viewers alike with their compelling stories and undeniable charm.

One of the most prominent examples of this trend in literature is the works of author Jasmine Guillory, whose novels consistently feature strong, independent black women as lead characters in interracial relationships. Books like *The Wedding Date*, *The Proposal*, and *Party of Two* have resonated with readers, as they showcase the lives and loves of successful, driven women who navigate the complexities of modern relationships with grace and determination. Guillory's characters, such as Alexa Monroe, Nik Paterson, and Olivia Monroe, have become beloved figures in the romance genre, capturing the hearts of readers with their wit, intelligence, and unwavering spirit.

In the bestselling interracial romance novel "Redefining Normal," author K.A. Holt offers a captivating example of a complex BWWM protagonist named Willow. Willow deals with societal expectations and challenges as a Black woman seeking love in a predominantly white world. Her story resonates with many readers due to its relatability, and it showcases the importance of creating characters that feel real and don't reinforce harmful stereotypes.

Similarly, in "Beyond the Black Stereotype," Author Farrah Rochon introduces readers to Dawn, a character who refuses to be defined by her race alone. She navigates the complexities of falling in love with a white man while balancing family and career. Rochon's detailed and authentic portrayal of Dawn's experiences allows readers to connect with her on a deeper level, further emphasizing the impact of complex, non-stereotypical characters.

In "A Black Woman in a Candlelit Room," bestselling author Farrah Rochon created a compelling and intricate BWWM protagonist in Dionne. As a successful businesswoman who challenges societal norms, Dionne finds herself in a vulnerable and authentic romantic journey. This portrayal demonstrates the significance of creating relatable and aspirational characters that challenge preconceived notions and inspire readers.

Take a look at the award-winning novel, "Opposites Atttract," by author Elizabeth J. Esta. Her multi-dimensional BWWM lead in Selena, a talented young singer who captures the heart of a foreign music producer named Alex. Selena's character is a beautiful blend of vulnerability, confidence, and ambition. The authenticity of Selena and Alex's relationship further emphasizes the need for non-stereotypical characters that resonate with readers.

Another author, Cat Johnson showcases the power of complex characters in her popular series, "The Donovans." Her ability to create diverse and well-rounded black heroine leads in a family of entrepreneurs facing the intricacies of interracial love highlights the importance of avoiding stereotypes and sculpting believable and relatable narratives.

Lastly, in "Before we Love," Author Adriana Anders wrote a compelling black female protagonist in Aurora. Through Aurora's journey of self-discovery and her experiences with interracial love, readers are exposed to an authentic, non-stereotypical experience.

* * *

Delicious Foods by Pen Hung Lee has captured the hearts of many readers with its richly developed and popular Asian protagonist, Anna. Anna is a Chinese-American refugee who glorifies the necessity of good food and the love it brings. Through Anna, Lee offers readers a relatable, culturally grounded character who overcomes adversity and embraces love. Moreover, Lee utilizes Anna's thoughts and memories to seamlessly weave together the entwined intricacies of food, identity, and relationships, further showcasing the importance of rich character development.

The character Binh-Minh, introduced in "The Brilliant World of Tomatoes by Matthew Do," is another excellent example of a well-liked Asian protagonist. Binh-Minh's story of self-discovery demonstrates the significance of character growth and the impact of love on personal transformation. Her strength, determination, and vulnerability captured the hearts of many readers, making her an unforgettable multicultural lead.

In "The Love that Split the World," American Book Award recipient, Ibi Zoboi, introduces readers to a thought-provoking, resilient, and charismatic black protagonist named Naledi. As a young refugee from South Africa, Naledi faces harsh realities when she is uprooted to the United States. The challenges Naledi undertakes, and the relationships she cultivates with both humans and nature, invite readers to delve deeply into her layers of complexity. Zoboi's devoted exploration of Naledi's story and character imbues the novel with a unique richness.

Let's not forget the world of televeision, shows like *Scandal* and *How to Get Away with Murder* had introduced audiences to powerful black female characters in interracial relationships. These series, both created by Shonda Rhimes, gave us iconic figures such as Olivia Pope and Annalise Keating, portrayed by Kerry Washington and Viola Davis respectively. These women had captivated viewers with their strength, brilliance, and ability to command any room they enter, all while navigating the ups and downs of their romantic lives with passion and determination.

Another notable example on TV is the character of Letitia "Leti" Lewis, played by Jurnee Smollett, in the series *Lovecraft Country*. Leti's interracial relationship with Atticus Freeman, played by Jonathan Majors, serves as a central plot point in the show, showcasing the power of love and connection in the face of adversity. Leti's strength, courage, and unwavering loyalty to those she loves have made her a standout character, capturing the hearts of viewers and cementing her place as a compelling and unforgettable figure in the world of television.

Movies like *Belle* and *A United Kingdom* have brought historical interracial romances to life, introducing audiences to remarkable black female characters who defied societal norms and fought for love against all odds. In *Belle*, Gugu Mbatha-Raw portrays Dido Elizabeth Belle, a mixed-race woman in 18th-century England who captures the heart of a white lawyer and navigates the complexities of their relationship with grace and determination. Similarly, in *A United Kingdom*, Rosamund Pike brings to life the character of Ruth Williams, who falls in love with and marries Prince Seretse Khama of Botswana, played by David Oyelowo, in a story that showcases the power of love to overcome even the greatest of obstacles.

The presence of black and brown lead female characters in interracial romances has not been limited to English-language media. International films and television series have also showcased diverse women in cross-cultural relationships, captivating audiences with their unique stories and perspectives. From the Brazilian telenovela *Lado a Lado* to the French film *Divines*, these characters have brought a fresh and compelling perspective to the world of romance, showcasing the beauty and complexity of love across different cultures and backgrounds.

The black and brown female characters in these interracial romances have become more than just fictional figures; they have become icons and role models, inspiring readers and viewers with their strength, resilience, and unapologetic pursuit of love and happiness. Their stories have resonated with audiences, showcasing the power of love to transcend boundaries and bring people together in the face of adversity.

The examples mentioned not only illustrate the importance of creating rich and multifaceted characters but also shed light on the various strategies writers employ to accomplish this goal. Establishing compelling and captivating characters—with complexity, depth, solidity, and vibrancy—entices readers and establish a connection that fuels their appreciation for the story.

Chapter 8

Backstories

When writing a BWWM romance, you must invest time and effort into building rich, authentic backstories for your main characters. These backstories will serve as the foundation upon which your characters' personalities, motivations, and relationships are built. By delving deep into their pasts, you can create multi-dimensional characters that readers will connect with and root for throughout the story.

To begin, consider the upbringing of your black female protagonist. Was she raised in a loving, supportive family or did she face challenges and adversity growing up? Perhaps she grew up in a single-parent household, learning the value of hard work and determination from her mother who worked tirelessly to provide for the family. Or maybe she was raised by her grandparents, absorbing their wisdom and stories of resilience in the face of discrimination. These early experiences will shape her outlook on life and her approach to relationships.

Next, turn your attention to your white male love interest. What was his childhood like? Did he grow up in a privileged, sheltered environment or did he face his own set of obstacles? Maybe he was raised by open-minded parents who taught him the importance of equality and acceptance, setting the stage for his willingness to pursue an interracial relationship. Alternatively, he could have grown up in a more conservative family, struggling to break free from the prejudices and expectations placed upon him. This internal conflict can add depth and complexity to his character.

As you flesh out your characters' backstories, consider their education and career paths. Your black female protagonist may have excelled academically, earning scholarships and degrees that opened doors to a successful career. This achievement could be a source of pride for her, but also a point of contention if her partner's family or social circle undervalues her accomplishments. Similarly, your white male character's career choices can provide insight into his values and priorities. Is he driven by ambition and success, or does he prioritize making a positive impact on the world?

Don't forget to explore your characters' past romantic relationships and how they have influenced their current outlook on love. Perhaps your black female protagonist has been hurt by previous partners who couldn't see past her race, leading her to be cautious and guarded in new relationships. Or maybe she had a positive, long-term relationship that taught her the importance of communication and compromise. Similarly, your white male character's past experiences with love can shape his expectations and fears in this new, interracial relationship.

It's also crucial to consider how your characters' racial identities have impacted their lives and worldviews. For your black female protagonist, this may include experiences of discrimination, microaggressions, and the constant pressure to prove herself in a society that often undervalues black women. She may have developed a strong sense of pride in her blackness, as well as a keen awareness of the challenges she faces in navigating a predominantly white world. By contrast, your white male character may have had to confront his own privilege and biases, learning to listen and empathize with his partner's experiences.

Another aspect to consider is your characters' hobbies, interests, and passions. These elements can provide common ground for your characters to bond over, as well as opportunities for growth and learning. Maybe your black female protagonist is an avid reader, finding solace and inspiration in the works of black female authors like Maya Angelou and Toni Morrison. Your white male character could be a music enthusiast, exposing her to new genres and artists that broaden her horizons. By sharing their passions, your characters can deepen their connection and understanding of each other.

As you develop your characters' backstories, don't shy away from including moments of pain, loss, and vulnerability. These experiences can be powerful catalysts for growth and change, allowing your characters to evolve and mature over the course of the story. Perhaps your black female protagonist has lost a family member to police brutality, fueling her passion for social justice and her determination to create a better world for future generations. Or maybe your white male character has struggled with addiction or mental health issues, learning valuable lessons about resilience and self-care that he can share with his partner.

Throughout the process of building your characters' backstories, it's essential to approach the task with empathy, sensitivity, and a willingness to learn. Research the experiences of real-life interracial couples and the challenges they face, as well as the joys and triumphs they share. Read works by black female authors and listen to the voices of black women in your community. By immersing yourself in these perspectives, you can create characters that feel authentic, relatable, and deeply human.

Ultimately, the key to building compelling backstories for your main characters in an interracial BWWM romance is to treat them as fully realized individuals, with their own hopes, fears, dreams, and flaws. By investing time and care into looking into their pasts, you lay the groundwork for a love story that transcends racial boundaries and resonates with readers on a profound, emotional level. Remember, the most memorable and impactful romances are those that feature characters who feel like real people, with histories and experiences that shape who they are and how they love.

Chapter 9

Authentic Dialogue

When writing an interracial romance, writing authentic, engaging dialogue is crucial to making the relationship and characters feel real and relatable to readers. You want the conversations to reflect the unique dynamics, shared and differing life experiences, and genuine connection between the protagonists. As romance author Farrah Rochon advises, "Dialogue is one of the most important elements of any book, but especially in romance. It's our primary insight into the characters' personalities." ("The Importance of Dialogue in Romance Novels"). By writing dialogue that rings true, you can create a love story that relates to readers on both sides.

One key aspect is ensuring the characters have distinct voices that suit their backgrounds. "Give each character a unique voice. The way they talk, the words they use, the rhythm of their speech - it all plays into making them feel like real, multi-dimensional people," suggests bestselling author Kristen Ashley. ("5 Dialogue Tips for Writing Vibrant Characters in Romance"). For the Black female character, consider her cultural upbringing, education level, profession and how those factors influence her communication style. Maybe she code-switches depending on the situation, is particularly expressive, or uses certain slang with friends and family. The White male lead's speech patterns would also reflect his own background and life experiences. Avoid stereotypical language for either character.

It's important the dialogue touches on the interracial aspect of their relationship in an organic way. "An interracial romance shouldn't feel like a wooden after-school special on racism. Let issues of race, prejudice, and cultural differences come up naturally when appropriate," says author Alisha Rai. ("How to Write An Interracial Romance"). Perhaps the couple discusses privileged versus marginalized experiences, has disagreements stemming from their different racial perspectives, or faces microaggressions from others when out together. But these issues should flow from the plot and characters arcs, not feel shoehorned in.

At the same time, don't feel obligated to focus heavily on race. "While it's important to acknowledge the realities of racism and cultural differences, an interracial relationship isn't only defined by overcoming hardship. There's a lot of joy, fun, and simple human connection too," notes author

Kennedy Ryan. ("Writing Interracial Romance Novels: A Conversation"). Show the couple having light, playful banter, intimate heart-to-hearts, and conversations about their hopes, dreams, and vulnerabilities like any other fictional duo. Fully flesh out their bond beyond racial lines.

Romantic dialogue should have an undercurrent of attraction, even in casual moments. "In a romance novel, every bit of dialogue is an opportunity for building sexual and emotional tension," says Brenda Jackson, who has published over 100 novels. ("Heat Up Your Romance Novel's Dialogue"). Maybe the Black heroine gets flustered by her White love interest's intense eye contact, or verbal flirtations. He might be hyperaware of the musicality of her voice or the appealingly straightforward way she communicates. Weave subtle, sensual details into their conversations.

Conflict is a natural part of relationships and leads to compelling dialogue. "Disagreements, fights, and emotionally charged conversations are like a pressure cooker for character development and relationship arcs in romance," says author Beverly Jenkins. ("Keeping Conflict Fresh in Romance"). Perhaps the couple faces internal conflicts about their cultural differences, or argues about experiencing the world differently because of racial inequality. Just make sure they always fight fair, using healthy communication rather than below-the-belt jabs.

Balance serious conversations with more light-hearted, everyday dialogue. "A common mistake is trying to pack too much drama or meaning into every single conversation between the romantic leads. In reality, couples spend a lot of time talking about mundane things too," points out author Jasmine Guillory. ("The Balance of Believable Dialogue in Romance Writing"). Show the pair chatting and bantering about their shared interests, joking around, and having silly disagreements. Perhaps the Black heroine gently teases the White hero about his questionable music taste or cooking skills.

Gradually evolve their dialogue over the course of the story to reflect their deepening bond. "The way a couple communicates should noticeably change from the early days of awkward first dates to established relationship status," advises romance editor Esi Sogah. ("The Art Of Writing Dialogue"). In the beginning, the couple might make more small talk, trip over their words, and tentatively discuss issues of race. As their connection grows, they talk more openly, finish each other's sentences, and aren't afraid to be vulnerable about cultural matters.

Make sure to give both characters equal opportunity to express themselves. "A pet peeve of mine in romance novels is when one character consistently dominates the conversation while the other just listens or reacts," says Alyssa Cole, an award-winning interracial romance author. ("Why Consent and Equality Must Be Present in Romantic

Dialogue"). Avoid falling into stereotypical gender roles like the Black woman constantly needing to be the Strong Sassy One or the White man always mansplaining things. Let them take turns leading dialogues and supporting each other verbally.

Pay attention to what isn't being said as much as what is. "So much of human communication is nonverbal - facial expressions, body language, meaningful silence. Those details add subtext to the couple's conversations," recommends author Rebekah Weatherspoon. ("It's Not What You Say, It's How You Say It: Subtext in Dialogue"). Describe the Black female protagonist narrowing her eyes thoughtfully as she listens, or the White male lead stumbling over his words endearingly when flustered. Beats of charged silence can be as impactful as a heartfelt speech.

Read the dialogue aloud to make sure it sounds natural. "One of the best ways to check if your dialogue works is to hear it spoken. If possible, have someone else read the other character's lines," says Vanessa Riley, a Regency-era BWWM romance author. As you verbalize the conversations, notice any places that feel too formal, out-of-character, or melodramatic. Adjust accordingly, using contractions and sentence fragments when appropriate. The words should flow effortlessly.

Get feedback on the dialogue from sensitivity readers or beta readers in interracial relationships. "It's invaluable to have readers from the backgrounds and experiences you're representing review your work before publication, especially when dealing with sensitive topics like race," advises author Kwana Jackson. ("Working With Sensitivity Readers As An Author"). They can help you ensure the interracial couple's discussions about their cultural differences are respectful and ring true, not inadvertently problematic. Consider their input carefully during the revision process.

Above all, focus on creating engaging dialogue that makes readers fall in love with the interracial pair and invest in their happily ever after. "At the end of the day, memorable romantic dialogue reveals who the characters are, makes us feel their chemistry, and convinces us this couple belongs together," says Stacey Abrams, who has written eight romance novels under the pen name Selena Montgomery. ("What Makes A Romance Novel Unforgettable"). Craft conversations that sparkle with wit, intimacy, and authenticity - the kind of words that linger sweetly in a reader's mind long after the last page.

Chapter 10

Avoiding Overused Tropes & Cliches

When writing an interracial romance, it's crucial to avoid overused tropes and clichés that can undermine the authenticity and depth of your story. You want to create a narrative that feels fresh, nuanced, and respectful, not one that relies on tired stereotypes or superficial representations of race. As romance author Jasmine Guillory points out, "Interracial relationships in fiction often fall into the same predictable patterns. It's important to subvert those expectations and explore the unique complexities of each couple." ("Reimagining Interracial Romance in Fiction"). By steering clear of these common pitfalls, you can craft an interracial love story that truly resonates with readers.

One of the most pervasive clichés in interracial romance is the "white savior" trope, where the white character rescues or uplifts the character of color from their struggles. "This trope is problematic because it perpetuates the idea that people of color need white people to save them, and it minimizes their agency and strength," explains author Kwana Jackson. ("Troublesome Tropes in Interracial Romance"). Instead of falling into this pattern, show both characters as equals who support and empower each other. Let the character of color have moments of strength, resilience, and problem-solving that aren't dependent on their white partner's intervention.

Another overused trope is the "tragic biracial character" who feels torn between two worlds and never truly belongs. "Mixed-race characters in romance are often portrayed as eternally conflicted and angsty about their racial identity, without any nuance or resolution," says author Rebekah Weatherspoon. ("Moving Beyond the Tragic Biracial Trope"). While it's important to acknowledge the challenges biracial individuals may face, avoid reducing them to this single dimension. Give your biracial character a fully developed personality, interests, and storyline beyond their racial identity crisis. Show them finding joy, pride, and belonging in their unique heritage.

Be cautious of the "interracial relationship as rebellion" cliché, where the couple's primary motivation for being together is to defy societal norms or family expectations. "When an interracial relationship is framed solely as an act of rebellion, it can trivialize the genuine love and connection between the characters," warns author Alyssa Cole.

("The Problem with Rebellion Romance"). While it's realistic to address the social pressures and disapproval interracial couples may face, don't let it be the defining factor in their relationship. Focus on developing their emotional bond, shared values, and personal compatibility beyond the rebellious allure of crossing racial lines.

The "colorblind romance" trope, where the characters claim not to see race at all, is another cliché to avoid. "Colorblindness might seem like a well-intentioned sentiment, but it actually erases the real experiences and cultural heritage of characters of color," advises author Farrah Rochon. ("Why Colorblindness Has No Place in Romance"). Instead of having your characters ignore or downplay their racial differences, let them openly acknowledge and appreciate what makes each other unique. Show them learning about and respectfully engaging with each other's cultural backgrounds, not pretending they don't exist.

Steer clear of the "white character as cultural guide" trope, where the white partner takes on the role of explaining or introducing their own culture to the character of color. "This trope can come across as condescending and implies that the character of color is ignorant or disconnected from their own heritage," says author Vanessa Riley. ("Subverting the Cultural Guide Stereotype"). Instead, show both characters as knowledgeable and well-versed in their respective cultures. Let the character of color take the lead in sharing their own traditions, experiences, and perspectives with their partner.

Another cliché to avoid is the "interracial relationship fixes racism" trope, where the couple's love is portrayed as a simple solution to deep-seated societal issues. "While interracial relationships can certainly challenge prejudice on an individual level, it's unrealistic and oversimplifying to suggest they can single-handedly dismantle systemic racism," notes author Beverly Jenkins. ("The Limits of Love in Fighting Racism"). Acknowledge the real-world challenges and discrimination interracial couples face, but don't position their relationship as a panacea for racism. Show them grappling with these issues in a nuanced, ongoing way rather than neatly resolving them.

Be mindful of the "fetishization" trope, where characters of color are exoticized or reduced to racial stereotypes by their white partner or the narrative itself. "Fetishization dehumanizes characters of color and turns them into objects of fascination rather than fully realized individuals," warns author Alisha Rai. ("The Danger of Fetishization in Romance"). Avoid describing characters of color in exoticizing terms or having their white love interest pursue them solely because of their race. Focus on developing their multi-dimensional personalities, interests, and desires beyond racial lines.

The "white character as cultural appropriator" trope, where the white partner adopts elements of their love interest's culture in a superficial or disrespectful way, is another pitfall to avoid. "Cultural appropriation is a sensitive issue that requires careful handling in interracial romance," advises author Naima Simone. ("Navigating Cultural Appropriation in Fiction"). Show the white character appreciating and learning about their partner's culture in a respectful, substantive way rather than merely mimicking it for cool points. Have them listen more than they speak, and defer to their partner's expertise and boundaries around cultural matters.

Avoid the "love conquers all" cliché, where the couple's feelings for each other magically overcome any societal or interpersonal obstacles related to race. "While it's important to show the power of love, it's equally important to acknowledge the real challenges interracial couples face and the ongoing work required to maintain a healthy relationship," says author Kennedy Ryan. ("The Myth of Love Conquering All"). Show the couple having honest conversations about race, facing microaggressions or discrimination together, and supporting each other through the ups and downs. Emphasize that their love is strong, but not a fairy tale that erases the realities of racism.

Another trope to be cautious of is the "white character as cultural voyeur," where the white partner's primary interest in their love interest stems from a fascination with their exotic "otherness." "This trope reduces the character of color to a cultural curiosity rather than a fully developed individual," warns author Stacey Abrams, who has written romance under the pen name Selena Montgomery. ("The Problem with Cultural Voyeurism"). Make sure the white character's attraction to their partner is based on their unique personality, shared interests, and emotional connection, not just a superficial interest in their cultural background.

It's also important to avoid the "post-racial utopia" trope, where the fictional world is portrayed as a place where racism no longer exists, and interracial relationships are universally accepted. "While it's tempting to imagine a society free from racial prejudice, it's important to acknowledge the ongoing realities of racism and the challenges interracial couples face," advises author Adriana Herrera. ("The Danger of Post-Racial Fantasies"). Ground your story in a realistic social context, even if it's not the primary focus. Show the couple navigating the complexities of race and racism in their relationship and the world around them, rather than erasing these issues altogether.

Finally, be cautious of perpetuating the "exceptional minority" trope, where the character of color is portrayed as unusually attractive, successful, or assimilated compared to others of their race. "This trope can reinforce harmful stereotypes and suggest that only certain types of people of color are worthy of love and acceptance," warns author Kwana Jackson. ("Deconstructing the Exceptional Minority Myth"). Make sure your characters of color are well-rounded individuals with a range of strengths and flaws, not just idealized representations of their race. Avoid implying that they are desirable partners because they transcend negative stereotypes about their racial group.

By actively subverting these common tropes and clichés, you can create an interracial romance that feels authentic, nuanced, and respectful. Focus on developing your characters as multi-dimensional individuals, exploring the unique dynamics of their relationship, and grounding their story in a realistic social context. As author Jasmine Guillory reminds us, "There are infinite ways to write a compelling interracial romance. The key is to approach it with creativity, sensitivity, and a commitment to telling a story that feels true to the characters and the world they inhabit." ("Reimagining Interracial Romance in Fiction"). By avoiding these overused tropes and having a fresh, thoughtful narrative, you can create an interracial love story that resonates with readers and expands the boundaries of the genre.

Chapter 11

Implementing Subplots and Character ARCs

When writing an interracial romance, implementing subplots and character arcs can add depth, complexity, and realism to your story. You want to create a narrative that goes beyond just the central love story, exploring the characters' individual journeys, conflicts, and growth. As romance author Jasmine Guillory notes, "Subplots and character arcs are essential for creating a well-rounded, engaging story. They give readers a reason to invest in the characters beyond their romantic relationship." By weaving in these additional layers, you can craft an interracial romance that feels rich, nuanced, and satisfying.

One effective way to incorporate subplots is to explore the characters' personal and professional lives outside of their romantic relationship. "Giving your characters goals, challenges, and passions that exist independently of their love story can make them feel more authentic and relatable," suggests author Rebekah Weatherspoon. For example, you could show the character of color navigating workplace discrimination or pursuing a dream career, while their white love interest grapples with family expectations or a personal creative project. These subplots not only add dimension to the characters but also provide opportunities for them to support and challenge each other in ways that deepen their bond.

Another important subplot to consider is the characters' relationships with their families and communities. "Interracial couples don't exist in a vacuum; they are shaped by their social and cultural contexts," notes author Kwana Jackson. Show how the characters' families react to their interracial relationship, whether with acceptance, disapproval, or a mix of both. Explore how the couple navigates cultural differences and expectations within their respective communities. These subplots can create tension, conflict, and opportunities for growth that stretch beyond the central romance.

Consider using subplots to address social and political issues that affect interracial couples. "Romance novels don't have to be purely escapist; they can also engage with real-world challenges and injustices," argues author Beverly Jenkins. Perhaps your story includes a subplot about the couple confronting systemic racism, participating in activism, or grappling with the complexities of privilege and oppression. These subplots can add depth and relevance to your story while still maintaining the emotional core of the romance.

Character arcs are another crucial element to implement in your interracial romance. "A character arc is the internal journey a character goes through over the course of the story, as they learn, grow, and change," explains author Alyssa Cole. For the character of color, their arc might involve learning to love and accept themselves fully, healing from past traumas, or finding their voice in a world that often silences them. The white character's arc could explore unlearning internalized biases, confronting their own privilege, or becoming a better ally. These individual journeys can intersect and influence the couple's relationship in meaningful ways.

One way to develop character arcs is through the use of internal conflicts. "Internal conflicts are the doubts, fears, and insecurities that characters grapple with throughout the story," says author Vanessa Riley. For example, the character of color might struggle with imposter syndrome or the pressure to be perfect in a society that often stereotypes them. The white character might battle guilt over their privileged background or fear of disappointing their family by pursuing an interracial relationship. By facing and overcoming these internal conflicts, the characters can experience profound personal growth.

External conflicts can also shape character arcs in interracial romances. "External conflicts are the obstacles and challenges that characters face in the world around them," notes author Adriana Herrera. These conflicts might include discrimination from others, cultural misunderstandings, or societal pressures that strain the interracial relationship. By confronting these external conflicts together, the characters can deepen their bond, learn to lean on each other, and grow stronger as individuals and as a couple.

Subplots and character arcs can also be used to subvert stereotypes and expectations in interracial romances. "It's important to challenge assumptions and give characters the space to surprise readers," advises author Alisha Rai. Perhaps the character of color is the one who comes from wealth and privilege, while the white character grows up in a working-class family. Maybe the couple defies gender norms in their relationship dynamics or career paths. By flipping the script on what readers might expect, you can create a more nuanced, thought-provoking story.

Another way to implement subplots and character arcs is through the use of secondary characters. "Secondary characters can provide support, challenges, and new perspectives that enrich the main couple's journey," suggests author Naima Simone. A supportive best friend, a wise family member, or even an antagonistic coworker can all play a role in shaping the characters' individual arcs and the subplots they navigate. These secondary characters can offer advice, create obstacles, or model different ways of being in an interracial relationship.

It's important to ensure that subplots and character arcs are well-integrated into the overall narrative. "Subplots should never feel like distractions from the main story; they should enhance and complicate it in meaningful ways," warns author Kennedy Ryan. Make sure each subplot and character arc ties back to the central themes and conflicts of the romance. Use them to raise the stakes, deepen the emotional resonance, and ultimately bring the characters closer together.

When implementing subplots and character arcs in interracial romances, it's crucial to approach them with sensitivity and authenticity. "Do your research, listen to voices from the communities you're representing, and strive to tell stories that feel true to the characters' experiences," advises author Stacey Abrams, who has written romance under the pen name Selena Montgomery. Make sure the challenges and growth the characters face are grounded in the realities of navigating an interracial relationship in a society that is still grappling with racism and prejudice.

Ultimately, subplots and character arcs are powerful tools for creating an interracial romance that feels deep, dynamic, and emotionally satisfying. "By giving your characters rich inner lives and meaningful challenges to overcome, you invite readers to invest in their journeys and root for their happily ever after," says author Jasmine Guillory. As you craft your story, consider how you can use these elements to explore the complexities of love, identity, and social justice in an interracial context. The result will be a romance that lingers in readers' hearts and minds long after they turn the final page.

Chapter 12

Connecting Setting to Character Development

Connecting the setting to character development is a powerful tool for creating a rich, immersive story. The setting can shape the characters' experiences, perspectives, and growth in profound ways. As bestselling author Beverly Jenkins notes in her book "Destiny's Embrace," set in 19th-century California, "The land and the people who inhabited it were as much a part of the story as the love that grew between the hero and heroine" (Jenkins 23). By intertwining the setting with the characters' journeys, writers can add depth, nuance, and authenticity to their interracial romance.

One way to connect setting to character development is by exploring how the characters navigate the social and cultural landscape of their environment. In "The Boyfriend Project" by Farrah Rochon, set in contemporary Austin,

Texas, the heroine, Samiah, grapples with being one of the few Black women in her tech workplace. Rochon uses the setting to highlight the microaggressions and isolation Samiah faces, as well as the supportive community she finds in her friendships with other women of color. As Rochon explains in an interview, "I wanted to show how the setting can both challenge and empower the characters in their personal and professional lives" (Rochon, "On Writing 'The Boyfriend Project'"). By grounding the characters' experiences in the specific social dynamics of their environment, writers can create a more nuanced, realistic portrayal of interracial relationships.

Another effective way to connect setting to character development is through the use of sensory details and imagery. In "The Proposal" by Jasmine Guillory, set in Los Angeles, the author uses vivid descriptions of the city's sights, sounds, and flavors to immerse readers in the characters' world. From the bustling food scene to the vibrant art galleries, the setting becomes a character in its own right, shaping the protagonists' experiences and interactions. Guillory explains in an essay, "I wanted readers to feel like they were right there with the characters, experiencing the city through their eyes and falling in love alongside them" (Guillory, "The Role of Setting in 'The Proposal'"). By engaging readers' senses and bringing the setting to life, writers can create a more immersive, emotionally resonant story.

The setting can also be used to challenge and subvert characters' assumptions and biases. In "Party of Two" by Jasmine Guillory, set in Berkeley, California, the heroine, Olivia, is a successful lawyer who has always played by the rules. When she falls for a charming white senator, Max, she must confront her own internalized beliefs about interracial relationships and power dynamics. Guillory uses the progressive, intellectual setting of Berkeley as a backdrop for Olivia's personal and political awakening. As Olivia navigates the city's activist circles and engages in conversations about social justice, she begins to question her own assumptions and grow in her understanding of systemic racism. Guillory notes in an interview, "I wanted to show how the setting can push characters out of their comfort zones and challenge them to grow in unexpected ways." By using the setting to confront characters' biases and spark personal growth, writers can create a more thought-provoking, transformative story.

The setting can also serve as a source of conflict and tension in an interracial romance. In "Take a Hint, Dani Brown" by Talia Hibbert, set in a small British town, the heroine, Danika, is a Black academic who faces discrimination and microaggressions from her predominantly white colleagues and students. When she enters into a fake relationship with Zafir, a former rugby player of South Asian descent, they must navigate the town's gossip and prejudices together.

Hibbert uses the claustrophobic, insular setting to heighten the stakes and tensions of the characters' relationship. As Hibbert explains in an essay, "I wanted to explore how the setting can both bring characters together and push them apart, and how they must learn to lean on each other in the face of external pressures" (Hibbert, "The Power of Setting in 'Take a Hint, Dani Brown'"). By using the setting to create obstacles and challenges for the characters, writers can add depth and complexity to their interracial romance.

Another way to connect setting to character development is by exploring how the characters' cultural backgrounds shape their relationship to place. In "American Love Story" by Adriana Herrera, set in upstate New York, the hero, Patrice, is a Haitian-American professor who has always felt like an outsider in the predominantly white academia. When he falls for Easton, a white American prosecutor, he must navigate not only their cultural differences but also their conflicting relationships to the criminal justice system. Herrera uses the setting to explore themes of identity, belonging, and social justice, as the characters grapple with their own privileges and marginalization. As Herrera notes in an interview, "I wanted to show how the characters' cultural backgrounds and experiences of place shape their worldviews and their approach to love and relationships" (Herrera, "Writing Authentic Interracial Romance"). By grounding the characters' development in their cultural contexts and relationships to place, writers can create a more nuanced, culturally specific story.

The setting can also be used to highlight the characters' shared and differing experiences of marginalization. In "The Voting Booth" by Brandy Colbert, set in Atlanta, Georgia, the protagonists, Marva and Duke, are both Black teenagers navigating the challenges of voter suppression and racial injustice. Colbert uses the setting to explore how the characters' shared racial identity shapes their political awakening and activism, even as they come from different socioeconomic backgrounds. As Colbert explains in an essay, "I wanted to show how the setting can both unite and differentiate the characters, and how they must learn to navigate their differences while fighting for a common cause" (Colbert, "The Role of Setting in 'The Voting Booth'"). By using the setting to highlight the characters' intersecting and diverging experiences of marginalization, writers can create a more intersectional, socially engaged story.

Another effective way to connect setting to character development is through the use of historical and cultural context. In "Wild Rain" by Beverly Jenkins, set in 19th-century Wyoming, the heroine, Rain, is a Black woman who has escaped slavery and built a new life as a successful businesswoman. When she falls for Spring, a Black man with a mysterious past, she must confront the ongoing legacies of racism and trauma in their community. Jenkins uses the historical setting to explore themes of resilience, healing, and the power of Black love in the face of oppression. As Jenkins notes in an interview, "I wanted to show how the characters' experiences are shaped by the historical and cultural context of their time and place, and how they draw strength from their ancestors and their community" (Jenkins, "Writing Black Love in Historical Romance"). By grounding the characters' development in the rich historical and cultural context of the setting, writers can create a more layered, meaningful story.

The setting can also be used to create a sense of familiarity and belonging for the characters. In "Real Men Knit" by Kwana Jackson, set in Harlem, New York, the hero, Jesse, is a Black man who has recently inherited his mother's knitting shop. As he struggles to keep the business afloat and win back his high school sweetheart, Kerry, he finds solace and support in the tight-knit community of Harlem. Jackson uses the setting to explore themes of family, legacy, and the power of Black-owned businesses in strengthening communities. As Jackson explains in an essay, "I wanted to show how the setting can provide a sense of rootedness and belonging for the characters, even as they navigate challenges and changes in their lives" (Jackson, "The Importance of Community in 'Real Men Knit'"). By using the setting to create a sense of familiarity and connection for the characters, writers can create a more emotionally resonant story.

Another way to connect setting to character development is by exploring how the characters' relationships to place evolve over time. In "You Had Me at Hola" by Alexis Daria, set in New York City and Los Angeles, the protagonists, Jasmine and Ashton, are both actors navigating the challenges of fame and cultural identity in the entertainment industry. As they fall in love on the set of a bilingual telenovela, they must confront their own fears and insecurities about belonging and success. Daria uses the dual settings to explore themes of ambition, authenticity, and the power of representation in media. As Daria notes in an interview, "I wanted to show how the characters' relationships to place evolve as they grow in their careers and their love for each other, and how they learn to find home in each other and in themselves" (Daria, "Writing Latinx Love in 'You Had Me at Hola'"). By exploring how the characters' relationships to place change and deepen over time, writers can create a more dynamic, emotionally satisfying story.

Ultimately, connecting setting to character development is a powerful tool for creating an interracial romance that feels authentic, nuanced, and emotionally resonant. As bestselling author Jasmine Guillory notes, "The setting is not just a backdrop for the characters' love story; it is an integral part of their journey, shaping their experiences, their growth, and their understanding of themselves and each other" (Guillory, "The Role of Setting in Romance"). By intertwining the setting with the characters' development, writers can create a story that explores the complexities of love, identity, and social justice in a specific time and place. Whether it's through sensory details, cultural context, or themes of belonging and marginalization, the setting can add depth, nuance, and emotional resonance to an interracial romance, making it a story that lingers in readers' hearts and minds.

Chapter 13

Concluding your Story

When concluding your romance novel, ensuring a satisfying and emotionally resonant conclusion is crucial. You want to leave your readers feeling fulfilled, hopeful, and invested in the characters' happily ever after. As romance author Jasmine Guillory advises, "The ending of a romance novel should feel like a warm hug, a promise that love can conquer all and that the characters have found their true home in each other" (Guillory, "On Writing Satisfying Endings"). By taking the time to craft a well-developed, emotionally impactful ending, you can create a story that lingers in readers' hearts and minds long after they turn the final page.

One key element of a satisfying ending is the resolution of the central conflict. Throughout your interracial romance novel, you've likely explored the challenges and obstacles that your characters have faced, both individually and as a couple. These conflicts might include external factors such as societal prejudice, family disapproval, or cultural differences, as well as internal struggles like self-doubt, fear of vulnerability, or unresolved trauma. In the ending, it's important to show how the characters have grown and changed through their journey, and how they've learned to confront and overcome these conflicts together. As author Beverly Jenkins notes in her book "Rebel," "The ending should demonstrate that the characters have not only found love, but also a deeper understanding of themselves and the world around them." By providing a clear and satisfying resolution to the central conflict, you can leave readers feeling a sense of catharsis and closure.

Another important aspect of a satisfying ending is the emotional payoff. Throughout your interracial romance novel, you've been building the emotional connection between your characters, showing how their love has deepened and evolved over time. In the ending, it's important to provide a culmination of that emotional journey, a moment of pure joy and connection that feels earned and authentic. This might be a grand romantic gesture, a heartfelt declaration of love, or a quiet moment of intimacy and understanding. As author Alyssa Cole describes in her novel "A Prince on Paper," "The ending should feel like a sigh of contentment, a recognition that the characters have found their true partner in life." By delivering a powerful emotional payoff, you can leave readers feeling satisfied and invested in the characters' happiness.

It's also important to tie up any loose ends and provide a sense of resolution for secondary characters and subplots. Throughout your interracial romance novel, you've likely introduced a cast of supporting characters who have played a role in the central love story. These might include family members, friends, colleagues, or even antagonists who have challenged the characters' relationship. In the ending, it's important to give these secondary characters their own sense of closure and resolution, whether that's through a reconciliation, a new opportunity, or a glimpse into their own happily ever after. As author Alisha Rai notes in her novel "Girl Gone Viral," "The ending should feel like a satisfying conclusion not just for the main characters, but for the entire world you've created." By tying up loose ends and providing a sense of resolution for secondary characters and subplots, you can create a more fully realized and immersive story.

Another key element of a satisfying ending is the sense of hope and possibility. In an interracial romance novel, the characters have often faced significant challenges and obstacles in their relationship, whether it's societal prejudice, cultural differences, or personal baggage. In the ending, it's important to show that their love has not only survived these challenges but has also given them the strength and resilience to face future obstacles together. As author

Rebekah Weatherspoon writes in her novel "Rafe," "The ending should feel like a beginning, a promise of all the adventures and joys that the characters will share in their life together." By infusing the ending with a sense of hope and possibility, you can leave readers feeling optimistic and inspired by the power of love.

It's also important to consider the pacing and structure of your ending. You don't want to rush through the resolution, but you also don't want to drag it out unnecessarily. As author Kwana Jackson advises in her book "Real Men Knit," "The ending should feel like a natural and satisfying conclusion to the story, not an afterthought or a rushed wrap-up." Take the time to build to the emotional climax, to show the characters' growth and decision-making, and to provide a clear sense of resolution and closure. At the same time, be mindful of the overall pacing and structure of your novel, ensuring that the ending feels proportional and well-integrated into the larger story arc.

Another consideration for the ending of your interracial romance novel is the balance between realism and escapism. While it's important to acknowledge the challenges and realities of interracial relationships in a prejudiced society, it's also important to provide a sense of hope and possibility. As author Jasmine Guillory notes in her novel "Party of Two," "The ending should feel true to the characters' experiences and the world they live in, but it should also offer a vision of love and happiness that transcends societal limitations."

Strike a balance between acknowledging the complexities of interracial relationships and celebrating the joys and triumphs of love.

It can also be effective to include an epilogue or a glimpse into the characters' future. This can provide readers with a sense of the characters' ongoing happiness and the lasting impact of their love story. As author Adriana Herrera writes in her novel "American Love Story," "The epilogue should feel like a satisfying glimpse into the characters' happily ever after, a confirmation that their love has only grown stronger and more resilient over time." Whether it's a flash-forward to their wedding day, a scene of domestic bliss, or a milestone moment in their future together, an epilogue can provide a final note of joy and satisfaction for readers.

It's important to stay true to your characters and their unique journey. Avoid generic or clichéd resolutions that feel disconnected from the specificity of your characters and their story. As author Talia Hibbert advises in her novel "Get a Life, Chloe Brown," "The ending should feel authentic and earned, a natural outgrowth of the characters' personalities, choices, and growth throughout the novel." By staying true to your characters and their individual arcs, you can create an ending that feels genuine and resonant.

It's also important to consider the overall theme and message of your interracial romance novel. What do you want readers to take away from your story? What larger truths or insights about love, identity, and social justice do you want to convey? As author Vanessa Riley notes in her novel "A Duke, the Lady, and a Baby," "The ending should feel like a culmination of the novel's central themes and messages, a powerful statement about the transformative power of love and the importance of fighting for a more just and equitable world." By weaving your larger themes and messages into the ending of your novel, you can create a story that feels not only emotionally satisfying, but also socially relevant and impactful.

Another consideration for the ending of your interracial romance novel is the role of community and support systems. In many interracial romance stories, the characters have had to navigate not only their own feelings and challenges, but also the reactions and expectations of their families, friends, and larger communities. In the ending, it can be powerful to show how the characters' love has not only transformed them as individuals, but also had a ripple effect on those around them. As author Farrah Rochon writes in her novel "The Boyfriend Project," "The ending should celebrate not only the characters' love for each other, but also the love and support of the communities that have nurtured and sustained them." By highlighting the role of community and support systems in the characters' happily ever after, you can create a more layered and emotionally resonant ending.

It's also important to leave readers with a sense of the characters' continued growth and evolution. While the ending of your interracial romance novel should provide a clear sense of resolution and happiness, it should also suggest that the characters' journey is not over. They will continue to learn, grow, and face new challenges and joys together. As author Nalini Singh writes in her novel "Rebel Hard," "The ending should feel like a promise of all the growth, discovery, and love that the characters will experience in their life together." By hinting at the characters' ongoing evolution and the future adventures they will share, you can create an ending that feels both satisfying and open-ended.

When revising and refining the ending of your interracial romance novel, it can be helpful to seek feedback from beta readers or trusted critique partners. Ask them if the ending feels emotionally satisfying, well-paced, and true to the characters and themes of your story. As author Cheris Hodges advises in her book "Rumor Has It," "The ending of your novel should be the culmination of all the hard work, heart, and vision you've poured into your story. Don't be afraid to revise and refine it until it feels just right." By seeking feedback and being open to revision, you can ensure that your ending is as polished and impactful as possible.

Ultimately, the ending of your interracial romance novel should leave readers feeling a sense of joy, hope, and emotional satisfaction. Through your characters' journey, you've explored the challenges and triumphs of love across boundaries of race, culture, and societal expectation. You've shown that true love has the power to transform individuals, relationships, and entire communities. As author Beverly Jenkins writes in her novel "Tempest," "The ending of a romance novel should be a celebration of love in all its forms - the love between partners, the love of family and friends, the love of community and justice. It should leave readers with a sense of the infinite possibilities of the human heart." By writing an ending that is emotionally resonant, thematically rich, and true to your characters and vision, you can create an interracial romance novel that will stay with readers long after they turn the final page.

In conclusion, ensuring a satisfying and emotionally resonant ending is a crucial part of writing a successful interracial romance novel. By resolving the central conflict, delivering an emotional payoff, tying up loose ends, and infusing your ending with hope and possibility, you can create a story that feels both authentic and uplifting. Remember to stay true to your characters, themes, and vision, and don't be afraid to revise and refine your ending until it feels just right. With care, attention, and heart, you can create an interracial romance novel that celebrates the power of love to transform lives and worlds.